William and the Hidden Treasure and Other Stories

Richmal Crompton, who wrote the original *Just William* stories, was born in Lancashire in 1890. The first story about William Brown appeared in *Home* magazine in 1919, and the first collection of William stories was published in book form three years later. In all, thirty-eight William books were published, the last one in 1970, after Richmal Crompton's death.

Martin Jarvis, who has adapted the stories in this book for younger readers, first discovered *Just William* when he was nine years old. He made his first adaptation of a William story for BBC radio in 1973 and since then his broadcast readings have become classics in their own right. BBC Worldwide have released nearly a hundred William stories on audio cassette and for these international best-sellers Martin has received a Gold Disc and the British Talkies Award. An award-winning actor, Martin has also appeared in numero͟͟ ͟͟ ͟͟ ͟͟ ͟͟ ͟͟ ͟͟ ͟͟lays, television series and films.

Titles in the *Meet Just William* series

William's Birthday and Other Stories
William and the Hidden Treasure and Other Stories
William's Wonderful Plan and Other Stories
William and the Prize Cat and Other Stories
William and the Haunted House and Other Stories
William's Day Off and Other Stories
William and the White Elephants and Other Stories
William and the School Report and Other Stories
William's Midnight Adventure and Other Stories

All *Meet Just William* titles can be ordered at
your local bookshop or are available by post
from Bookpost (tel: 01624 677237).

Meet Just William

William and the Hidden Treasure and Other Stories

Adapted from Richmal Crompton's
original stories by Martin Jarvis

Illustrated by Tony Ross

MACMILLAN CHILDREN'S BOOKS

First published 1999 by Macmillan Children's Books
a division of Macmillan Publishers Limited
20 New Wharf Road, London N1 9RR
Basingstoke and Oxford
www.panmacmillan.com

Associated companies throughout the world

ISBN 0 330 39100 3

11 13 15 17 19 18 16 14 12

A CIP catalogue record for this book is available from
the British Library.

Typeset by SX Composing DTP, Rayleigh, Essex
Printed and bound in Great Britain by
Mackays of Chatham plc, Chatham, Kent

Contents

Dear Reader

Ullo. I'm William Brown. Spect you've heard of me an' my dog Jumble cause we're jolly famous on account of all the adventures wot me an' my friends the Outlaws have.

Me an' the Outlaws try an' avoid our famlies cause they don' unnerstan' us. Specially my big brother Robert an' my rotten sister Ethel. She's awful. An' my parents are really <u>hartless</u>. Y'know, my father stops my pocket-money for no reason at all, an' my mother never lets me keep pet rats or <u>anythin'</u>.

It's jolly hard bein' an Outlaw an' havin' adventures when no one unnerstan's you, I can tell you.

You can read all about me, if you like, in this excitin' an' speshul new collexion of all my fav'rite stories. I hope you have a jolly gud time readin' 'em.

Yours truly

William Brown

William and the Hidden Treasure

"I'm going to be a millionaire when I grow up," announced William to the Outlaws. "I'll d'vide it with you three. We'll all be millionaires."

The interest of the others became less impersonal.

Then Henry said, "William, how're we going to start gettin' the money?"

William looked at him rather coldly.

"There's a hundred ways of gettin' to be millionaires. There – there's—" then a flash of inspiration "—there's findin' hidden treasure. Why, when you think what a lot of pirates and smugglers there must have been, the earth must be *full* of hidden treasure if you know where to dig. An' if you've got a map . . ."

They scuffled joyfully homewards down the lane, playing their game in which the sole object was to push someone else into the ditch. William was neatly precipitated into it by a combined attack from Ginger and Douglas.

Then they saw William sit up and take something from the hedge.

"What is it?"

"Bird's nest."

He was frowning thoughtfully. From among the moss and feathers he had taken a small piece of crumpled paper.

He spread it out.

"*Crumbs!*" he breathed. "It's a map, of hidden treasure!"

They all tumbled down into the ditch with him. The piece of paper was crumpled but the markings on it were quite plain.

There were two circles. Under one were the

words "Copper Beech", and under the other, the word "Cedar". And between the two circles – in the centre – was a large cross. At the bottom of the paper was written "P.M. 7.10".

"It's a *map*," said William. "Look at it. All yellow and old. I expect that the pirate what made it jus' threw it into the hedge when they were takin' him off to prison, an' it's been here ever since . . . The cross is where the treasure is, of course."

"I say," said Henry. "There's a copper beech an' a cedar tree in Miss Peache's garden. He must've buried it in Miss Peache's garden."

"Right," said William. "We've got to find the 'xact spot, an' dig for it. I bet it's not as easy as it looks. He must've put some catch in it, so's if anyone who wasn't his mother or wife found the map, they wun't be able to get hold of the treasure."

"What does 'P.M. 7.10' mean?" said Ginger.

3

"I guess that's the catch," said William gloomily.

"There were witches in those days, you know," said Henry, "an' I bet they used to get witches to put spells on maps of hidden treasure so's only the people they meant to find 'em could find 'em."

"Yes," agreed William. "P.M. 7.10. That's the spell. It means ten minutes past seven in the evening . . . it means you'll only find it if you dig for it at ten past seven. *That's* it!"

*

They met outside the gate of Miss Peache's house a little before ten past seven that evening, armed with various implements.

Exactly between the copper beech and the cedar was a rose-bed, which would considerably facilitate digging operations. They advanced cautiously across the lawn.

But Miss Peache, prim and middle-aged, was sitting writing at a desk at a window overlooking the lawn. They returned to the road.

"We'll jus' have to wait till she's not there," said William philosophically. "It doesn't matter which day we do it, so long as it's ten minutes past seven . . ."

There followed a week of daily disappointment.

"We've gotter get her away somehow," said William. "Get her away by ten minutes past seven one day, so's we can go an' find the treasure. We'll have to find out the sort of things she's int'rested in."

"It's dreams she's int'rested in," said

Douglas. "She writes about 'em in a magazine. I know 'cause I heard my mother talking about her the other day. And she's most int'rested in people who have *real* dreams, or somethin'."

"All right," said William, "then we'd better start havin' real dreams."

The next afternoon when Miss Peache emerged from her gate as usual at two-thirty, four boys were standing there.

She could not help noticing that one of them gave a violent start of surprise, and pointed her out to the others.

"What is the matter, little boys?" she said sharply. "Is – is there anything *strange* about me?"

"Oh, no," said one of them hastily. "Oh, no. It's only that – that I *dreamed* about you last night, an' I was so surprised to see you comin' out of the gate 'cause I din' know you were a real person. I thought you were only in a dream. I'm sorry," ended the ingenuous child smugly, "if I was rude."

"Not at all. This is most interesting. Am I – er – exactly like the lady in your dream?"

"'Xactly," said the boy earnestly, "but in my dream you hadn't got a coat on. You'd got a sort of – black dress with blue in it."

"B-but how amazing! I've *got* a dress like that. I was wearing it last night. *Do* tell me – where was I in your dream? Wait a minute."

And she took out her notebook.

"You were in a sort of room," said William slowly. "There was a sort of writing-table in the window, and bookcases all round the room, and there was a sort of big blue pot umbrella-stand in a corner of the room—"

"A Nankin vase, dear," said Miss Peache, as she scribbled hard in her little notebook. "But it's all most *amazing*. One of the most *wonderful* pieces of material that's ever come my way. Now what was I *doing* in your dream?"

"You were writing at the table," said William. "An' you put your pen in a sort of big silver inkpot."

"Yes, that was presented to me, dear boy, by the members of a little society I was once president of. A little society for the interpretation of dreams. It has always been a great treasure to me. I could not work at all without it. If it were not in its place there on my writing-table I should not, I am quite sure, be able to carry on my wonderful work at all. Now, what did I do next, dear boy?"

But it was at this point that the Outlaws had left their point of vantage near Miss Peache's window, to go home to bed.

"I woke up," said William simply.

"Dear, dear. Never mind." She closed her notebook. "Now I want you to come to me tomorrow and tell me exactly what you dream tonight. This is all most valuable material for me. It will form the basis of my next article."

"The thing to do," said William, after she had gone, "is to take away her inkstand. Then she won't be able to write, so p'raps she'll go out . . ."

So they crept through the bushes and snatched the inkstand from the table that stood at an open window.

But even this daring step was not successful. True, Miss Peache did not write. But neither did she go out.

She sat in her study ringing up the police station every five minutes to ask if they'd had any news of her inkstand yet, and receiving messages of condolence from her friends.

William went to Miss Peache the next morning, and described a dream in which

Miss Peache busied herself continually with the telephone and wept and wrung her hands.

"Dear boy," she said, "I *really* feel that perhaps you might *dream* where my dear inkstand is. Before you go to sleep tonight, you must concentrate on where my dear inkstand is . . ."

"Where are you goin' to dream she found it?" asked Henry.

"I know!" said William. "Mr Popplestone's house. I *know* she knows him, 'cause I saw them talkin' in the road. An' I know what his study's like, 'cause once I was in it with Father . . ."

Miss Peache listened to William's dream, open-mouthed.

"It's – it's simply *amazing*. You say that in your dream you saw me going into Mr Popplestone's *study*?"

"Yes, an' it was jus' ten minutes past seven by the clock on the mantelpiece."

"And I went to the cupboard in the wall and opened it?"

"Yes."

"And I found my beloved silver inkstand in it?"

"Yes, and found your b'loved silver inkstand in it."

"And did you, in your dream, infer that he'd *taken* it?"

"Er, yes," said William. "That's how it seemed to me. It seemed to me as if he'd taken it."

"I'd have said that he was the last person in the world to do a thing like that. But, his hobby of bird study. It may be a blind to cover his secret career. However – you said that the time by the clock was ten minutes past seven?"

"Yes," said William emphatically. "Ten minutes past seven . . ."

Concealed in the bushes, the Outlaws watched Miss Peache set off from her house. Then they crept forth on the lawn.

Outside in the road was the wheelbarrow

that they had brought to take the treasure home. They carried their spades and shovels.

William also carried the silver inkstand, which was to be slipped back on to Miss Peache's study table as soon as the treasure was found.

They stood solemnly by the rose-bed, and William took out the map.

"Here it is. An' we can see the church clock so the minute it gets to ten past seven we'll start diggin' . . ."

Socrates Popplestone sat at his desk in his study. He had spent an enjoyable day watching a couple of whitethroats, and had sat down with the intention of writing up his notes.

But he wasn't writing up his notes. He was thinking about Miss Peache. In fact, lately, he'd begun to feel quite sentimental about Miss Peache.

He'd picked up a glove that she'd left in church last Sunday, and was – well, treasuring it. He roused himself to begin his bird notes.

And then – a most amazing thing happened. The door opened and Miss Peache walked in.

She said, with dramatic quietness, "Mr Popplestone, you know what I've come for. I know you took it."

A flush of guilt dyed Mr Popplestone's cheek.

His hand went to the pocket where he was carrying her glove.

"Did the verger tell you?" he asked.

He'd had a suspicion all along that the verger had seen him take it.

"No," she said, in a voice of horror. "I'd no idea that he was party to it. Why did you take it?"

"Because it belonged to you," he replied.

She stared at him in amazement.

"I've been carrying it about all day next to my heart," he went on.

"Next to your h—? Did you take the ink out of it first?"

"I never noticed any ink in it."

"You *couldn't* carry it about all day next to your heart. It's too big."

"Too big?" he said tenderly. "If it fits your hand it can't be very big."

"But I never put my whole hand into it . . . Oh, but I know where it is. A supernatural manifestation has been vouchsafed to me through a little child . . ."

She walked over to the cupboard in the wall and flung it open. In it reposed a small pile of notebooks and a bottle of cough mixture.

Miss Peache looked taken aback, but then pointed an accusing finger at Mr Popplestone, and said sternly, "Where is it?"

"Here," said the guilty man. With hanging head he brought out a crumpled white glove from his waistcoat pocket.

"W-w-w-what's that?"

"Your glove. I took it on Sunday. I thought you said you'd come for it."

"Oh. I – I – I feel rather faint, Mr Popplestone."

"Please call me Socrates," he said as he dashed wildly to the cupboard and got out the bottle of cough mixture to restore her.

"Certainly," murmured Miss Peache, "and will you call me Victoria?"

Then, first making sure that they were ready to receive her, she fainted into his arms.

The betrothed pair entered the gate of Miss Peache's house. They had agreed to be married very quietly early the next year.

"You want *looking* after, Socrates,

dearest," said Miss Peache fondly. "Oh –
good gracious!"

They had turned the corner of the house,
and there on the lawn were four boys engaged
in digging up the rose-bed.

"Good gracious! Boys, what are you
doing?"

William had seen her, and with commend-
able presence of mind had thrust the silver
inkstand into the hole, covering it lightly with
soil.

He turned to her.

"I've had another dream: I fell asleep an' I dreamed that I dug up this bed an' found your inkpot, so I came straight along to try. I b'lieve I've got to it at last. Yes. Here it is."

"How *wonderful*!" breathed Miss Peache. She turned to her fiancé.

"*There.* You doubted the boy's veracity when I told you about him. But isn't this *proof*? And such a dear boy!"

Mr Popplestone looked at William. Then he put a half-crown into William's hand – a sort of thank-offering to fate.

The next day William and Ginger slipped quietly into William's mother's drawing-room, where visitors were being entertained.

They intended to hand round the cake-stand and, with a skill born of long practice, to abstract enough cakes from it for themselves and for Douglas and Henry, who waited outside.

There was *still* lots of time to get the

treasure. They knew where it was, anyway. The map was still in William's pocket.

A woman with red hair was saying, "Peggy Marsden told me to take down the date so that I shouldn't forget her birthday – and I did, but I lost the bit of paper. Trixie says it's the seventh of October.

"I remember now. I put down P.M. 7.10 on a bit of paper to remind me. It was the bit of paper I'd begun to design Gladys and John's new garden on. I'd only just begun. I'd given them a copper beech and a cedar tree, and a sundial just between them, and then Peggy came in and I made a note of her birthday on the paper and then lost it . . ."

William and Ginger crept brokenly out of the room. Brokenly they told the other two of the ruin of their hopes.

The four of them gazed sadly into the distance, watching their millionaire life vanish into thin air.

Then William took the half-crown from his pocket.

"Well," he said, "it's enough for one ice-cream an' ginger beer for us all, anyway."

It wasn't much to salvage from the wreck of their fortunes, but it was something.

William and the Snowman

The Outlaws were sitting gloomily in the Old Barn.

"Well, at least it's trying to snow," said Ginger. "It's years since it snowed properly. In all the books you read it snows at Christmas, but it never seems to in real life."

"We had a jolly good time last holidays," said Douglas.

"We'd got Brent House last holidays," William reminded him.

The summer holidays had consisted of a glorious possession of an empty house and garden. In fact William had said that their occupation of it was a kindness to its owner.

"We can't possibly do it any harm," he had said, "an' we'll keep it aired for him with breathin' in it."

It wasn't till they heard that Brent House was sold to a Colonel Fortescue that they stood back and surveyed their handiwork.

The result was depressing: broken windows, holes in the lawn, a damaged garden seat . . .

Colonel Fortescue, when he moved in, had soon tracked down the culprits and had executed severe punishment on William.

William had sworn to avenge this deadly insult. He had even appealed to his grown-up brother, Robert, to avenge him.

But Robert flatly refused and had become deeply enamoured of the Colonel's beautiful niece, Eleanor. But the Colonel was putting every obstacle in Robert's way. The Colonel disapproved of all Eleanor's suitors – except Archie, the son of an old friend.

And Archie had come to stay at Brent House for Christmas.

So affairs stood when Ginger said, "Never mind. I bet it'll snow tonight."

And Ginger was right. They woke up the next morning to find the ground thickly covered with snow.

Moreover, Robert had lost his voice and Mrs Brown, finding that his temperature was 101°, put him to bed and sent for the doctor.

William couldn't help feeling that it was a judgement on Robert for refusing to avenge him; and so it was with a blithe spirit that William set out to spend the afternoon with the Outlaws.

After an exhilarating snowball fight they decided to make a snowman. The result was, they considered, eminently satisfactory. The snowman was life-size and well proportioned, and his features, marked out by small stones, denoted, the Outlaws considered, a striking and sinister intelligence.

"Let's pretend he's a famous criminal, an' have a trial of him," suggested William.

The others eagerly agreed.

They stood in a row and William addressed him in his best oratorical manner.

"You're had up for being a famous criminal," he said sternly, "and you'd better be jolly careful what you say."

The snowman evidently accepted the advice, and preserved a discreet silence.

Then Ginger said, "Couldn't we get a coat an' hat for him? He looks so silly like that. You can't imagine him goin' into shops an' places, an' stealin' things, all naked like that."

24

"Yes," said William. "Tell you what! I'll get Robert's coat an' hat. He's in bed with a sore throat, an' he won't know. I'll go'n get 'em now."

The coat was a new coat of a particularly violent tweed that Robert had bought in a desperate moment, when he felt that he must do something to cut out the wretched Archie or die. Certainly when wearing the coat he was a striking figure.

William draped it round the shoulders of the snowman. The hat tilted slightly forward at a sinister angle over the stone eyes.

"Well," he said, "I bet he looks as much like a crim'nal as anyone *could* look. Now go on, Ginger."

But, as Ginger stepped forward, William interrupted him with, "Look!"

They looked at the path that led through the field, and there was Colonel Fortescue coming along slowly, his eyes on the ground. It was obvious that he had not seen them.

"Quick!" whispered William, retreating

into the shelter of the wood. "Make snow-balls for all you're worth."

He felt at last that Fate had delivered his enemy into his hands. By the time Colonel Fortescue had come abreast with them, they had a good store of ammunition.

"One, two, three – go!" whispered William.

The startled Colonel suddenly received – from nowhere, as it seemed to him – a small hail of snowballs. They fell on his eyes and ears, they filled his mouth, they trickled down his neck.

When the frenzy of the attack abated, he looked round furiously for the author of the outrage. Dusk was falling, but he plainly saw a figure in a coat and hat standing at the end of the field, near the wood. No one else was in sight.

The snowballs had come from that direction. There wasn't the slightest doubt in the Colonel's mind that the figure in the coat and hat had thrown them.

He strode across to it, trembling with rage.

The Colonel was short-sighted, but he knew that coat. It had dogged him in his walks with Archie and his niece. It clothed the form of the presumptuous Robert Brown, who dared to try to thwart his plans for his Eleanor's happiness.

"You impudent young puppy!" he said. "How dare you . . . You . . ."

Words failed him. He raised his arm and struck out with all his might.

Now a thaw had set in and Robert's tweed coat – which was very thick and warm – had completed the effect. As the Colonel struck the figure, it crumpled up, and lay, an inert mass, at his feet.

He gazed down at it through the dusk in horror; then, with a low moan, turned and fled from the scene of his crime.

The Outlaws crept out from hiding.

"Crumbs," said William. "We got him all right! Wasn't it funny when he knocked the snowman down? But, I say, I'd better be getting Robert's hat and coat back. Let's

take the snowman into the wood, too, then we can pretend we never had one here if anyone makes a fuss."

They bundled up Robert's hat and coat, and rolled what was left of the snowman into the wood. Before they could make their escape, however, they saw Colonel Fortescue returning through the dusk and hastily took shelter again.

The Colonel was not alone. Archie was with him. They both looked pale and frightened.

When they reached the spot where the snowman had been, they stopped, and the Colonel looked about him.

"Great heavens!" he said. "It's gone."

"What's gone?" said Archie.

"The corpse. I left it just here."

"It couldn't have gone. You couldn't have killed him."

"I did, Archie, I swear I did. He crumpled up and fell like a log. I must have hit some vital organ. Good heavens, what shall I do? I merely meant to teach him a lesson. I didn't want to kill him."

"You're sure it was Robert Brown?"

"Absolutely. I recognised his coat even before I saw his face."

"You couldn't have killed him, sir, or his body would have been here. He may have . . ."

"Crawled into the woods to die," supplied the Colonel wildly, "or crawled home. Archie, the police may be out looking for me now. I came straight back to you, Archie, because I knew you'd stick by me through thick and thin."

But Archie seemed to have views of his own on that subject.

"That's all very well, Colonel," he said. "I'm – I'm frightfully sorry for you and all that, but – well, but you can't expect me to mix myself up in an affair of this sort."

"You mean you won't stand by me, Archie?" said the Colonel pathetically. "Think of – Eleanor!"

"Honestly, sir, I've got my reputation to think of. No man can afford to be mixed up in a case of this sort. I'm sorry, Colonel, not to be able to stay over Christmas after all, but if things are as you say, you won't be wanting visitors. You may not even be at home to entertain them."

And the gallant Archie scuttled off through the snow, to pack his things. The Colonel turned and staggered brokenly away towards the Browns' house.

William, having heard all this, ran home by

a short cut, hung up Robert's hat and coat and slipped upstairs to Robert's bedroom to see how he was. Robert was asleep, but his mother, much touched by William's brotherly solicitude, said that the doctor had left him some medicine.

"He can't talk yet, of course," she said.

William went downstairs and waited at the front gate till Colonel Fortescue arrived.

"Robert's very, very ill," volunteered William.

Colonel Fortescue gave a gasp. "He's – he's got home?" he said.

"Oh yes," said William.

"Did he – did he crawl home?"

"I don't know. I didn't see him come home."

"Have – have they had the doctor?"

"Oh yes, they've had the doctor."

"And – does he think he'll live?"

"Yes, he seems to think he'll live all right."

"Er – what has he told the doctor about – about what happened to him?"

"He can't speak yet," said William truthfully.

"He's unconscious?"

"Yes," said William. "I've jus' been up to his room an' he's quite unconscious."

"But you're sure they think he'll live?"

"Oh yes, they think he'll live."

The Colonel heaved a sigh of relief.

"I'll go home now. I'll come round again in the morning."

The Colonel arrived next morning to find William waiting by the front gate.

"The doctor's been, an' Robert's a lot better today," said William.

"I'm glad," said the Colonel. "And – and now they know the whole story from him, what steps are they going to take?"

"They don't know anythin' from him," said William.

"What? Hasn't he told them anything?"

"No," said William, "he's not told them anythin'."

"Oh, noble fellow!" said the Colonel. "Noble fellow!"

"The doctor says he can come out for a little walk tomorrow," said William.

"Well, my boy, if you'll let me know what time he's coming out, I'd be grateful to you. And you may play in my garden any time you like."

He walked slowly down the road, and William turned four cartwheels to celebrate the final wiping out of the insult.

Next morning Robert, on emerging from the house for his walk, well muffled and wearing the famous tweed coat, was surprised to find the Colonel waiting for him.

The Colonel seized his hand and said, "Forgive me, my boy, forgive me. I – I've done you a terrible wrong."

Robert, remembering the snubs he had suffered at the Colonel's hands, quite agreed with him, but was ready to be generous.

"That's quite all right, sir," he said. "Please don't speak of it."

"I'm afraid I hurt you very much indeed," went on the Colonel.

"Well, sir, I can't say you didn't," said Robert, "but – but please don't speak of it."

"You're generous, my boy. Generous. Let me accompany you, my dear boy. Take my arm please."

Robert, rather bewildered by this sudden change of front, took the Colonel's arm, and making the most of the wholly unexpected situation, began by talking about Roman Britain – which he knew to be the Colonel's favourite subject.

The Colonel was enthralled. They reached Brent House, and the Colonel called Eleanor out to join them.

Mrs Brown, who was watching for their return, asked the Colonel and Eleanor to come in to tea.

"I'm so glad to find this boy so much better," said the Colonel.

"Yes, he's got over it very well," said Mrs Brown.

"Mrs Brown," he said, "I think that the time has come to tell you something that only Robert and I know."

Robert gaped at him. For one delirious moment he thought that the Colonel was going to publicly offer him Eleanor's hand.

"What only Robert and I know, Mrs Brown, is the cause of his recent severe illness."

"But I do know, Colonel," said Mrs Brown.

"You do?"

"Yes, his tonsils are too big. I can't think why, because neither mine nor his father's are any size at all to speak of."

36

"No, Mrs Brown," said the Colonel. "His tonsils are not too big. No, the truth is that on Monday afternoon, foolishly, perhaps, this young man snowballed me and, very, very foolishly, I knocked him down so violently I thought I had killed him."

He looked round the table. They were all gazing at him.

Only William was unmoved, his face wearing an expression of seraphic innocence.

"I – I – I – *snowballed* you?" gasped Robert.

"Yes, you young devil! And a jolly good shot you are, too."

"I – I – I swear I never snowballed you, sir," said Robert.

"Come, come, my boy. Better let me make a clean breast of it. You'll be denying that I knocked you down next!"

"Yes, sir," said Robert. "I certainly do."

"Good heavens!" said the Colonel. "You mean to say you've no memory of it at all? I'm afraid there must have been concussion."

But Mrs Brown assured the Colonel that Robert had been in bed on Monday afternoon.

"But, great heavens! I saw you as plainly as I see you now. Apart from everything else I knew your coat."

The Colonel turned to William.

"You said that he was unconscious."

"He was," said William innocently. "He was asleep. I thought that was what you meant."

"Well, it must have been a hallucination. A

hallucination sent me by Fate, to show me the utter worthlessness of one in whom I had trusted, and to show me the worth of one whom I had ignorantly despised."

He leant over and shook Robert warmly by the hand.

Robert grinned inanely, and then turned to meet Eleanor's eyes. They were smiling at him fondly. It was all too wonderful to be true. And yet it was jolly mysterious.

The old chap had said that he'd seen him as plainly as possible in his hat and coat. Snowballing him . . .

He looked at William.

William's face wore a shining look of innocence; his eyes were slightly upraised.

Robert knew the look well. That kid knew something about all this. He'd get hold of that kid tonight, and he'd— No, on second thoughts, Robert decided not to pursue any investigations that might alter the situation. He looked at William again.

The angelic solemnity of William's face

broke up – just for a second – then quickly restored itself . . .

The situation was highly satisfactory as it stood.

Violet Elizabeth Runs Away

"*Away from Civil'sation*," said William scornfully.

"It's a dotty subject."

"Ole Frenchie always gives dotty subjects for essays," said Ginger.

"Ole Frenchie's against civil'sation," said Douglas. "He says he wished he'd lived in the Stone Age."

"I wish he had, too," said William.

"He says," said Henry, "that when things get too much for him he likes to leave the horrors of civil'sation behind and make for the peace an' solace of the open countryside."

41

"Dotty sort of thing he would say," said William.

The four Outlaws had just reached the old barn when suddenly Ginger said, "Gosh, who's this?"

It was a strange figure, dressed in a shapeless trailing coat, the face almost hidden in a thick black mop of hair.

They gazed at it in bewilderment as it approached.

"Hello, William!" said a small shrill voice.

"Gosh!" groaned William. "Violet Elizabeth Bott!"

Violet Elizabeth removed the mop-like wig.

"Yes, it's me, William," she said with her habitual lisp. "I've run away from school."

"Run away?" said William.

"Yes," said Violet Elizabeth. "I don't like it. It's a nasty place and they give you nasty food. Mince!"

Violet Elizabeth's parents had gone abroad – Mr Bott on business and Mrs Bott on a trip to Paris – and they had parked Violet Elizabeth at Rose Mount School, a select boarding-school for girls on the outskirts of the village.

"But what on earth—?" said William, pointing to the wig that she was now dangling in one hand.

"It's a disguise," said Violet Elizabeth proudly. "I stole it. It's a wig. It belongs to one of the big girls, and I stole it for my disguise, so that I could run away. And the coat belongs

to one of the mistresses. I stole that for my disguise, too."

They stared at her helplessly.

"Yes, but what are you going to *do*?" said William.

"Stay with you," said Violet Elizabeth simply. "You must hide me so that they can't find me."

"Well, we *can't*," said William indignantly.

"But you must, William. They're nasty people at that school. I wouldn't eat mince and they said I mustn't have anything else to eat till I'd eaten it, so I shall starve to death if you send me back."

She looked at him appealingly.

"You can't send me back to starve to death, William. It would be the same as *murdering* me. And if you try to take me back, I'll *scream* an' I'll *scream* an' I'll *scream* till I'm sick, I will."

William turned to the others. "Gosh! What are we goin' to *do* with her?"

"Take her back," said Ginger.

William gave an ironic snort.

"Yes, screamin' and yellin' all down the road! That's a *jolly* good idea, I *mus'* say!"

"She bites, too," said Douglas. "She's got teeth like daggers. She bit me once an' it took *days* to get well."

"It's a sort of moral problem," said Henry.

"What d'you mean, moral problem?" said William.

"Well, she's sort of taken sanctuary with us."

"What's that?" said William. "Same as a bird sanctuary?"

"Yes, in a way," said Henry, "but it's more *serious* with humans. She's come an' asked for sanctuary an' we've got to give it to her. It would be *treachery* to hand her over to her enemies. She's – trusted us, you see. She's taken *sanctuary* with us."

"Yes, I s'pose there's somethin' in that," said William, "but we can't hide her up for the rest of our lives. An' she's fussy about food. She'd start screamin' and carryin' on."

"She's a sort of mixture of an orphan an' a refugee," said Douglas. "It makes it jolly difficult."

Violet Elizabeth had tripped over her coat and fallen at William's feet. She put the wig on again, peering up at them through the tangle of dark hair.

"It's a lovely disguise, isn't it?" she said.

"Now listen, Violet Elizabeth," said William. "You're a mixture of an orphan an' a refugee, same as Douglas says, an' we can't keep you 'cause we've nowhere to hide you, an' we can't take you home 'cause your mother's gone on a trip to Paris."

"The fairground of Europe," said Henry. "That's what I once heard someone call it."

"Yes," said Violet Elizabeth with sudden bitterness. "She's in Paris, riding on round-abouts and swinging on swings at this fairground and she doesn't care what happens to me. She just leaves me to be *poisoned* by mince an' starved to death. I won't go back to her at all now, an' it'll serve her right."

"Well, we can't go on keepin' you for the rest of our lives," said William. "It would be like that man what had to go about with an albatross tied round his neck."

Violet Elizabeth glowered at them through the forest of black hair.

"I'm not going to that nasty school," she said.

Then what could be seen of her face broke into a beaming smile.

"I *tell* you what I'll do. I'll get myself adopted. I'm sick of school an' I'm sick of my own mother. I want a nice new school and a nice new mother, so you must get me adopted."

"How could we?" said William.

"Put a notice in the post office," said Violet Elizabeth.

The Outlaws hesitated.

"Well, it's better than jus' stayin' here," whispered William to Ginger. "We'll get rid of her somehow."

They reached the post office and stood for

a minute outside, examining the notices that were displayed in the window.

They went in. It was empty except for the post mistress, who looked at them without interest.

"Well?" she said. "What can I do for you?"

"We want to put a card in the window," said Violet Elizabeth.

"Where is it?" said the post mistress.

"We haven't got one," said William. "If we tell you what we want, will you write it down?"

"What is it?" said the post mistress.

Violet Elizabeth cleared her throat impressively.

"Loveable young lady," she said, "wants to be adopted by nice person."

"All right," said the post mistress. "Now off you go, and no more of your nonsense!"

"We'll have to think of something else, then," said Violet Elizabeth when they reached the crossroads.

"Well, we can't stay here," said Douglas. "Anyone might come along an' we'd all get into a row. Look! Someone's comin' now!"

Mrs Monks and Miss Caruthers were coming down the road, deep in conversation.

"Quick!" said William, diving into the overgrown ditch. The others followed. The two women stopped at the crossroads and stood talking.

"You see," said Miss Caruthers, "this friend of mine who shall be nameless – this friend of mine wanted to find a little girl to bring up as a companion for her own little girl, who's an only child and needs companionship . . .

"Well, I got in touch with someone who seemed ideal – a widower with a little girl of the right age. I got the interview all fixed up . . . This friend of mine (who shall be nameless) is staying at the Somerton Arms in Marleigh . . .

"Anyway, I was going to take the child to the interview there this afternoon. Then I heard from the widower by this morning's post that the whole thing has fallen through.

"I've been called to the sick-bed of a dear aunt and have to rush off to the train. I tried to ring my friend up at the hotel but couldn't get through to her . . .

"I wrote a note for the gardener to take but he's not turned up. Well, there's nothing I can do about it, now. So provoking."

"I'm sorry I can't help," said Mrs Monks, "but the Women's Guild committee is waiting for me and I'm late already. Goodbye."

"Oh well," said Miss Caruthers with a sigh. She stood irresolute for a moment. Suddenly she brightened. She had caught sight of a boy's head in the ditch.

"Boy!" she called.

Slowly, William emerged.

Miss Caruthers had not lived in the neighbourhood long enough to distinguish one boy from another. Here was a boy, she felt, who could be trusted.

"Will you do something for me, boy?" she said.

"Uh-huh," said William guardedly.

Miss Caruthers took a note from her handbag.

"Will you go to the Somerton Arms at Marleigh and deliver this note for me? Here's sixpence for your trouble."

William crammed the note into his pocket, and received the sixpence into a grubby palm.

"Thanks," he said, "but—"

But Miss Caruthers was already scurrying away.

The other four climbed out of the ditch.

"That's what I want to be," said Violet Elizabeth, beaming joyfully. "I want to be the little girl's companion. I'll have a nice new friend, an' a nice new mother. It's just what I want. She'll be waiting for me now and she'll never know I'm not the real one. Come on. Let's go to Marleigh quick."

They stared at her.

"Well, it's a way of gettin' rid of her," said William. "We can jus' take her there an' leave her."

He opened his hand.

"Look! She gave me sixpence."

"You must buy me a lolly then," said Violet Elizabeth, "to stop me starving to death."

"All right," said William. "If we buy you a lolly, will you promise to go back to school straight away?"

"I'll think about it," said Violet Elizabeth graciously.

Ginger ran back to the shops and returned with a lollipop.

"Now will you go back to school?" said William, handing it to her.

"No," said Violet Elizabeth, "I said I'd think about it and I've thought about it and I've decided not to."

Violet Elizabeth had dropped her lollipop on to the road, but she picked it up and proceeded to lick the dust off it.

"*Look* at her!" said Ginger. "Turns up her nose at mince an' eats dust!"

"I don't mind the taste of dust," said Violet Elizabeth. "It's quite *clean* dust. And I made up all that about the mince. I wanted to run away from school so I made all that up about the mince to give me a reason for running away. It was clever of me, wasn't it?"

"Oh, come on," said William. "Let's take her to that place an' get rid of her."

They trailed over the fields to Marleigh and the Somerton Arms.

"I'm going to have a nice new mother," said Violet Elizabeth complacently. "My own mother doesn't care for anything but riding on roundabouts in Paris, so I don't want her any more."

Mrs Bott was not riding on roundabouts in Paris. She was sitting in her bedroom at the Somerton Arms, dressed up to the nines, awaiting her visitor.

During the last few months Mrs Bott had been planning fresh manoeuvres to force her way into the ranks of the local aristocracy.

The aristocracy had been to Paris. They came back with Paris outfits and Paris hats. Mrs Bott had never been to Paris, so when Mr

54

Bott went to Holland on business, and decorators had taken possession of the Hall, she decided to seize the opportunity.

But her thoughts had turned more and more frequently to Violet Elizabeth at Rose Mount School. To judge from her letters, Violet Elizabeth was not happy at Rose Mount School.

Wandering through the Paris shops, Mrs Bott came to the conclusion that the root of the trouble was the fact that Violet Elizabeth was an only child. What Violet Elizabeth needed was a little companion.

She decided to move secretly. She wrote to Miss Caruthers because Miss Caruthers was a newcomer to the village who could be trusted not to spread the news.

She decided to leave Paris at once, to come home incognito, as it were, and stay quietly at the Somerton Arms till her husband had returned and the decorations at the Hall were completed.

Then she would blossom forth in all her

Paris glory. She had had things done to her face and to her hair. She had bought a Paris dress and a Paris hat.

She was wearing both hat and dress now as she sat in her bedroom in the Somerton Arms awaiting the little companion.

There was a knock at the door and the manageress of the hotel entered, closing the door behind her. She looked pale and shaken.

"There's a child," she said. "At least I think it's a child. Something about you expecting her . . ."

"Oh yes," said Mrs Bott, moving the hat sideways. "I'm expecting her. Show her in."

She opened the door and a small figure entered. The wig hid her face completely and the lollipop dangled from it, inextricably entangled in the thick black hair. The coat followed like a bedraggled tail. Mrs Bott gave an hysterical scream.

"Go away, you horrible child!" she cried. "I wouldn't let my Violet Elizabeth *see* you even. It would *kill* her. Go away!"

But, at the same moment, Violet Elizabeth had also given an hysterical scream; and heard not a word of this.

"I don't *want* you for my mother, you nasty woman! I want my own nice mother. I want my own Mummy. Go away, you nasty horrid woman! If you don't go away I'll scream and I'll scream and I'll *scream* . . ."

Mrs Bott stared at her. The voice lisping was familiar. The scream was familiar. What she could see of that small distorted face was familiar.

"Oh, my darling!" she said, throwing herself on the floor beside Violet Elizabeth.

"Go away!" screamed Violet Elizabeth again.

Mrs Bott's abrupt descent had not only displaced Violet Elizabeth's black wig, but had also displaced the Paris hat and hairdo – reducing her, almost, to her old self.

"Oh *Mummy!*" said Violet Elizabeth. "My own *nice* Mummy!"

They sat on the floor clasped in each other's arms.

And then Miss Golightly, Headmistress of Rose Mount School, entered: she had tracked her errant pupil to the Somerton Arms. Mrs Bott rose to her feet.

"Miss Golightly," she said sternly, "you have a lot to explain."

Miss Golightly explained it. The flu epidemic had reduced the staff to half its normal numbers and things had, she admitted, got a little out of hand. But that a pupil of Rose Mount School should run away was unprecedented.

She fixed a stony gaze on Violet Elizabeth.

"And *you*, Violet Elizabeth," she said, "have something to explain. Kindly explain it."

Violet Elizabeth's small sweet face wore a look of troubled innocence. "It wasn't my fault," she said plaintively. "It was those horrid boys. They made me do it."

"What boys?" said Miss Golightly.

The manageress had joined the group in the bedroom.

"There were four boys at the door . . ." she said.

But the four boys were at the door no longer. They had heard fragments of the conversation and they were following Old Frenchie's example – leaving the horrors of civilisation behind them and making for the peace and solace of the open countryside.

William Goes Shopping

"William, dear," said Mrs Brown, "I wonder if you'd do something for me this afternoon. I'll give you a shilling if you will."

William immediately assumed an expression of shining selflessness.

"It's all right, Mother," he said. "I'll help you any way I can."

"That's very sweet of you, dear," said Mrs Brown, deeply touched. "It's this," she went on. "I forgot to order the fish for dinner, and I want you to go into Hadley and get it for me. From Hallett's in the High Street. I'll write down on a piece of paper just what I want you to get."

William said, "Will you give me the shilling before I go, then I can spend it in Hadley?"

"Certainly not, dear. I shall only give you the shilling if you bring it back properly. Unless you bring it back properly I shan't give you a penny."

"S'pose," he said thoughtfully, "s'pose that I do it *nearly* all right, will you give me sixpence?"

But Mrs Brown, who had finally come to the conclusion that a penny and his bus fare would have been quite enough, answered, "Of *course* not, William. I shan't give you anything at all unless you do it *perfectly*, and a shilling's far too much in any case . . ."

It was an hour later. William was sitting on the grass near the top of the hill that led down to Hadley. He was trying for the hundredth time, without success, to make a whistle.

No need, of course, to hurry. There was only the fish to get, and he needn't be back before tea-time.

He took up his penknife again, and began to cut the hole a little wider. Perhaps that was what was wrong.

He blew – not a sound. He felt that life would hold no more savour for him if he couldn't find out how to make whistles.

Suddenly he heard a voice behind him.

"An' what are ye trying to do, young sir?"

He turned around.

An old man sat on a chair outside a cottage door. So intent had William been upon his whistle that he had not noticed him before.

"Make a whistle," he said and returned to his attempts.

"It's the wrong way," quavered the old man. "Ye'll never make a whistle that way."

William wheeled round. "D'you know how to make a whistle?"

"Aye. 'Course I do," said the old man. "I were the best hand at makin' a whistle for miles when I were your age. Let's look at it now . . ."

He inspected William's abortive efforts at whistle-making with unconcealed contempt.

"Ye'll never make a whistle this way. Never. Where's your sense, boy?"

"I dunno. I – I sort of thought that was how you did it."

"Tch! Tch!" said the old man. "What on earth are boys coming to? I'd've bin ashamed at your age! I would for sure."

"Could you show me how to do it?"

"How can I! Now you've cut it about like this? You'll have to get me another reed. Quickly."

"I don't know where there are any," said William.

"Tch! Tch! I don't know what boys are coming to. Through that stile, across the field. You'll find them growing by the river. Why, when I was a boy—"

But William had already vaulted the stile. He returned panting a few minutes later with an armful of reeds.

The old man was waiting for him with his penknife. William handed him a reed, and he began to cut it at once.

"This way . . . an' then that . . . don' make the hole too big . . . I wish I'd got my ole dad's penknife. An' I *ought* to have it by rights too."

"Now, Dad," said a woman's voice from inside the cottage. "Don't start on that again."

"All very well sayin' don' start on that again," said the old man. "I *ought* to have my ole dad's penknife by rights. He'd promised it to me. Charlie always wanted it too, but my ole dad he promised it to me, an' left it to me in his will."

A middle-aged woman came to the cottage door.

"Yes, he left it to you in his will, and you lost it."

"I did *not* lose it," said the old man, beginning to shape another whistle. "I lent it to Charlie an' he never give it me back."

"He says he did an' you lost it."

"No," said the old man. "Others have seen it up there, behind his shop. He keeps it on his desk. Makes a joke of it to 'em. He says I can have it if I'll come for it. If I'd got the use of my legs . . . I tell you, that penknife—"

"I'm sick to death of hearing about the penknife," said the woman, and went back into the cottage, slamming the door.

The old man went on talking and whittling.

"You don' find any knives like my old dad's now. A great big one of horn, with his 'nitials on. Charlie borrers it an' never gives it me back. Always like that, he was. From a boy. Cunnin' . . . If I'd got the use of me legs, he wouldn't have dared. I'd've gone down to his shop an' had it off him. Now have a blow at that an' see if it's all right."

William had a blow. It certainly was all right.

"Now you make one all yourself," he said to William.

He watched eagerly, as if the fate of both of them depended upon the result. When finally William, almost trembling with suspense, raised the whistle to his lips and blew a shrill blast, he clapped his gnarled hands and chuckled again.

"Fine!" he said. "Fine! Now, that's a proper whistle, that is. Shameful – warn't it? – to think of a boy of your age not being able to make a whistle. Hundreds of them I've made, with my old dad's knife when I was a boy. Oh, when I think of that Charlie havin' it – well—"

"Where does he live?" asked William.

"Got a little tobacconist's in the High Street next to the boys' outfitters. Well, now you can make a whistle, can't you?"

"Yes," said William, and blew another piercing blast.

He walked up the road to the High Street as light-heartedly as if he trod air. He could make whistles. He saw himself in the future, making hundreds and hundreds of whistles. He'd teach Ginger and Douglas and Henry. They'd all make whistles . . .

And his heart overflowed with gratitude to his benefactor . . . His old dad's penknife . . .

William began to examine the shops he passed. A tobacconist's, yes, and next door to it a boys' outfitters. William stood still. No one was passing. He peered into the tobacconist's shop. It was empty. He tiptoed in. But no one appeared.

Summoning all his courage, he tiptoed to the doorway of the inner room. It was empty. In the corner by the window was an old-

fashioned desk, and on it was an enormous ancient horn penknife.

William's eyes gleamed. He darted forward, seized it, then turned to run back to the road. But then he heard an angry shout behind him, and knew that someone had come running down a small flight of stairs.

He leapt through the shop to the street. The door of the boys' outfitters next door was open. William plunged into it. A bald-headed man was fast asleep in a chair behind the counter. He stirred. He was obviously about to open his eyes.

William looked about him desperately. He pulled aside a curtain and leapt into the shop window where stood a row of wax models about his own size wearing tweed shirts.

He snatched a label: "Latest Fashion 63s." from the nearest, pinned it on to his own suit, and took his place at the end of the row.

Immediately afterwards, just as the bald-headed man was opening his eyes, a short stout man plunged through the doorway.

The bald-headed man looked at him sternly.

"What on earth's the matter?" he said indignantly. "Anyone would think the place was on fire."

"A boy," panted the stout man. "In my back room . . . chased him out . . . came in here . . ."

The bald-headed man looked about him. "Nonsense!" he said. "No boy's been in here."

"I saw him. I tell you, I *saw* him."

"Very well. Find him, then. I've seen no boys."

The stout man went into the inner room, and then came out again.

"No," he said. "He doesn't seem to be anywhere here."

"He probably went next door," said the outfitter. "I don't believe there ever was a boy."

But Charlie had already gone next door.

William, standing to attention among the row of models, holding his breath, was beginning to feel more and more ill at ease. The bald-headed man was fully awake now, and sat barring his only way of escape. At any time he might be discovered.

He had taken advantage of the fluster of Charlie's entry, to seize a large straw hat from the floor near him and put it on his head, dragging it down over his eyes.

William scanned the passers-by fearfully from beneath the brim, standing very still, trying not to breathe. One woman, who held a little girl by the hand, stopped and looked at the models attentively. William could hear their comments.

"Well," she said, "I don't think much of the suit the end one's got on, do you, Ermyntrude?"

"Naw," said the little girl.

"It's not a suit *I'd* like to pay sixty-three shillings for."

"Naw," said Ermyntrude. "And its 'at's too big."

"Not what they used to be – none of these shops."

Ermyntrude was bending down in order to see under the large brim. "It's gotta nugly face too."

"Well, they can't 'elp their faces," said the woman. "They make 'em with wax out of a sort of mould, and when the mould gets old the faces begin to come out odd. An' sometimes they get a bit pushed out of shape."

"This one's mould was old," said Ermyntrude, "an' pushed out of shape, too, I should think."

"Yes. Come on, love. We'll never get the shoppin' done at this rate."

They passed on. William was heaving a sigh of relief when he saw that half a dozen small boys were flattening their noses against the glass.

"They're dead boys," one of them was saying in low fearful tones. "I know they're dead boys. My brother told me. The shopman goes out after dark catchin' 'em.

"Then when he's killed 'em he dresses 'em up and puts 'em in his shop window. If you was to come past his shop after dark he'd get you.

"My brother said so. My brother once met him after dark carryin' a sack over his shoulder . . ."

They gazed with awe and horror. Suddenly the smallest boy gave a scream of excitement.

"*Oo!* Look! Look at the one at the end, the one with the hat. He forgot to put new clothes on that one. It's got its old ones on."

They contemplated William in tense silence.

Then the smallest one said, "It's *breathin'*. Watch it! It's *breathin'*! It's not dead."

They gazed at this phenomenon, open-mouthed. William, though trying to retain immobility, found the spectacle of their noses flattened to whiteness against the glass irresistibly fascinating.

"Look!" said the smallest one again, craning his head to look under the hat. "It's movin' its eyes too. I can see it movin' its eyes. It's comin' alive! It's comin' alive! They do sometimes. Moths do sometimes after you've put 'em in a killin' bottle."

"Go an' tell him it's comin' alive," said another.

"*You* go'n tell 'im."

At this moment the hat slid forward. Instinctively, William caught it and replaced it on his head.

Seeing that the situation was completely lost, he relieved his feelings by pulling his most hideous face at the row of gaping spectators, and then put out his tongue.

"*Oo!* G'n, tell him quick. It's coming alive. It'll get away in a minute."

The smallest boy put his head into the shop, and called out, "I say, mister! One of them boys in the window's comin' alive—"

With a roar of fury the proprietor rushed after them. They fled before him down the street. Seizing his opportunity, William leapt from the window, out of the shop and sped along the road and up the hill.

The old man still sat outside his cottage door. William flung him the penknife as he passed. The old man's voice followed him on his headlong flight.

"Me old dad's penknife! Glory be! Me old dad's penknife!"

The bus was waiting at the top of the hill, and William leapt upon it, just as it started off.

A quarter of an hour later, he was walking jauntily homewards. He'd had a jolly exciting afternoon, and he'd learnt how to make whistles.

He put his hand in his pocket and encountered a mysterious envelope with something hard inside. He took it out and opened it. Money. Money? What on earth—?

And then suddenly he remembered. Hallett's. The fish. The errand he'd gone into town for. He'd forgotten all about it.

The shilling. He'd been going to have a shilling for it. It was too late to go back now. He entered the house slowly with a sinking heart. His mother came out of the drawing-room.

"Oh, William darling, I'm *so* sorry. I *quite* forgot that Hallet's was closed this afternoon," she said. "I remembered as soon as you'd gone."

William tried to assume the expression of one who had gone on an errand to a shop and found it closed.

"Did you feel very cross with me, darling?" went on his mother.

"No," said William. "No, not at all, Mother."

"Well, we're going to have omelettes instead of fish, dear, so it's all right. And you've brought the money back?"

He handed her the money.

"You can have the shilling, of course, dear, just as if you'd done it, because it was only the accident of the shop being closed that prevented you. *And* another sixpence because it must have been so annoying for you."

William swaggered down the road, his whistle at his lips, emitting blasts with every breath. One hand was in his pocket, lovingly fingering his shilling and his sixpence.

First he'd go to Mr Moss's sweet shop and buy some bull's eyes, big 'uns. Then he'd meet the other Outlaws and teach them how to make whistles.

Life seemed to stretch before him – one glorious opportunity for whistle-making.

He gathered breath and blew a piercing blast – a paean of exultation and triumph and joy of life.

Meet Just William
Richmal Crompton
Adapted by Martin Jarvis
Illustrated by Tony Ross

Just William as you've never seen him before!

A wonderful new series of *Just William* books, each containing four of his funniest stories – all specially adapted for younger readers by Martin Jarvis, the famous "voice of William" on radio and best-selling audio cassette.

Meet Just William and the long-suffering Brown family, as well as the Outlaws, Violet Elizabeth Bott and a host of other favourite characters in these six hilarious books.

Richmal Crompton
Just William and Other Animals

*"You can't have another dog, William," said Mrs Brown firmly,
"you've got one."*
"Well it's at the vet's, an' I want a dog to be goin' on with."

William has a certain affinity with members of the animal
kingdom. In fact, some would say that William is rather like
his furry friends. And he would do anything to help an animal
in distress (unless it's a cat).

Champion of canine causes, defender of innocent rodents,
avenger of bestial wrongs – no tormentor of rats or pups is
safe when William Brown is around . . .

Ten classic stories of William – and other animals.

"Probably the funniest, toughest children's books ever written"
Sunday Times

Richmal Crompton
Just William at Christmas

Christmas is a time for peace, joy and goodwill. But William's presence has never been known to enhance the spirit of the season.

Whether he's wrecking the Sunday School's carol singing outing, standing in as Santa Claus for the Old Folk, or making a Christmas plant pot out of Ethel's hat, William somehow manages to spread chaos wherever he goes.

Ten unforgettable stories of William at Christmas, with the original illustrations by Thomas Henry.

Collect all the titles in the
MEET JUST WILLIAM series!

The prices shown below are correct at the time of going to press.
However, Macmillan Publishers reserves the right to show new retail
prices on covers which may differ from those previously advertised.

William's Birthday and Other Stories	0 330 39097 X	£3.99
William and the Hidden Treasure and Other Stories	0 330 39100 3	£3.99
William's Wonderful Plan and Other Stories	0 330 39102 X	£3.99
William and the Prize Cat and Other Stories	0 330 39098 8	£3.99
William and the Haunted House and Other Stories	0 330 39101 1	£3.99
William's Day Off and Other Stories	0 330 39099 6	£3.50

All *Meet Just William* titles can be ordered from our website,
www.panmacmillan.com, or from your local bookshop
and are available by post from:

Bookpost
PO Box 29, Douglas, Isle of Man IM99 1BQ

Credit cards accepted. For details:
Telephone: 01624 677237
Fax: 01624 670923
E-mail: bookshop@enterprise.net
www.bookpost.co.uk

Free postage and packing in the United Kingdom